# HECATE

## A NEW GRAPHIC NOVEL BY JOHN LAWRY

In the previous chapter* Hecate was forced to leave her
home after she exposed and destroyed a paedophile
ring that had been supported by her local government
Now wanted by the corrupt police she encounters an
strange pair of adventurers who start her on a journey
through exotic places and times and finally into the
world of the ancient Egyptian Gods

(*Chapter one in LEGION 1 )

ISBN978-0-6481710-4-1

CHAPTER TWO

THE KINGS HEAD

SOME FOOD AND A BEER PLEASE
THAT WILL BE FIVE PENCE ...MADAM?

GOOD MORNING MAY I HAVE SOME WATER FOR THE CAT PLEASE

YOU TWO WITH THE CIRCUS THEN? A LADY IN MENS' CLOTHES AND A BOY WITH A PET TAME LION!
YAWN
I THINK HE'S A PUMA, NOT A LION HE'S NOT MINE, I SAW HIM OUTSIDE AND SOMEHOW KNEW HE WAS THIRSTY...
OH.. HE MIGHT BE TAME, I DON'T REALLY KNOW
IT'S TIME TO LEAVE WITCH
IT'S TIME TO LEAVE BOY

CRASH!
IT HAS BEEN REPORTED THAT SOMEONE HAS A DANGEROUS WILD ANIMAL IN HERE
WE ARE HERE TO ARREST THE PERSON AND TO PUT DOWN THE ANIMAL
SARGE, SARGE... THAT'S THE WITCH FROM THE CITY, SHE GOT AWAY FROM THEM
I ARREST YOU TOO. YOU WILL BE RETURNED TO YOUR FATE!
AH! SO YOU ARE HERE TO CAST YOUR BLACK SPELLS!

WUMP!
QUICK! RUN..

WELL DONE WITCH GIRL... I WOULD HAVE HAD TO RIP THEIR FACES OFF
IT WAS YOU.. YOU PUT WORDS INTO MY HEAD
IT'S NOT HARD ..MOST HUMANS HAVE SO MUCH SPACE IN THERE
LET US GO INTO THE WOODS, I HAVE A BOON TO ASK OF YOU

MY MISTRESS SENT ME TO EUROPE, LOOKING FOR SOMEONE WITH YOUR SKILLS AND POWER
SENT YOU FROM WHERE, WHY?..
FROM THE MOTHER NILE..FROM EGYPT.. MY MISTRESS HAS SEEN THE OLD GODS ARE STARTING TO FADE AWAY
A GOD DRAWS THEIR STRENGTH FROM THE BELIEF OF THEIR PEOPLE, WITHOUT BELIEF THEY DIE
SHE WANTS YOU TO TELL HER WHAT IS GOING TO HAPPEN IN THE FUTURE...
I CAN'T DO THAT! THINGS CAN CHANGE, NO FUTURE IS SET!
YOU CAN!..YOU CAN SUMMON AAMON, HE CAN SHOW THE REAL FUTURE
SUMMON A DEMON! NO! THEY ARE ALL UGLY AND HAVE BAD MANNERS!
AH..EXCUSE ME.. THERE ARE MEN COMING WITH DOGS REALY BIG DOGS!
WOO WOO WOO
WOOF
BUT YOU MUST.. I CAN PUT US OUT OF TIME TO HIDE US, IF I DON'T THE HUNTERS WILL CATCH YOU..THIS TIME YOUR PINK POWDER WON'T SAVE YOU BOTH

I THINK I'M BEING BLACKMAILED BUT OKAY..

THERE!

NOW! TOUCH MY COAT

BLIP!

WHERE ARE WE? AND WHY AM I HERE ANYWAY?
WE ARE IN A SPACE BETWEEN MOMENTS, OUT OF TIME AND THE WORLD
AND AS UNLIKELY AS IT SEEMS I FEEL YOU HAVE A ROLE TO PLAY, LATER!
BUT TIME IS PASSING..AFTER ALL I'M BREATHING AND MY HEART IS BEATING
NO..IN HERE NO TIME IS PASSING, YOUR MIND IS CREATING THE SENSE OF TIME SO YOU FEEL OK
FOLLOW ME, WE MUST GO AT LEAST A LEAGUE FROM HERE ELSE WHEN WE GO BACK WE WILL BE KILLED.. WE WOULD RETURN TO THE SAME MOMENT WE LEFT

WE HAVE WALKED FOR 7500 OF YOUR HEARTBEATS, SO WE CAN RETURN TO TIME
WOMP
NOW WE ARE IN A SAFE PLACE WITCH GIRL.. BEGIN YOUR SUMMONING

VERY WELL, I'LL NEED A SMALL FIRE..
UT FACERENT SECUNDUM VERBUM: ET VOCAVI VOS ET A JURAMENTO QUOD AD NOS AAMON APPARESIT. UT FACERENT SEC.....
WHAT DO YOU WANT LITTLE HEDGEWITCH?
BOOF!

SHOW ME THE FUTURE, WHAT FATE BEFALLS MY MISTRESS BASTET
GET OUT OF MY HEAD PUSSY CAT! YOU CAN'T CONTROL ME!
AND I KNOW WHAT WILL BEFALL YOUR KIN LITTLE PUMA... AFTER 10 MILLION YEARS ON THIS PLANET YOU WILL BE ALL DEAD IN 600 YEARS, EXTINCT AT THE HANDS OF THE HUMANS YOU HELP
NO, HE CAN'T CONTROL YOU BUT I CAN! NOW SHOW HIM WHAT HE SEEKS

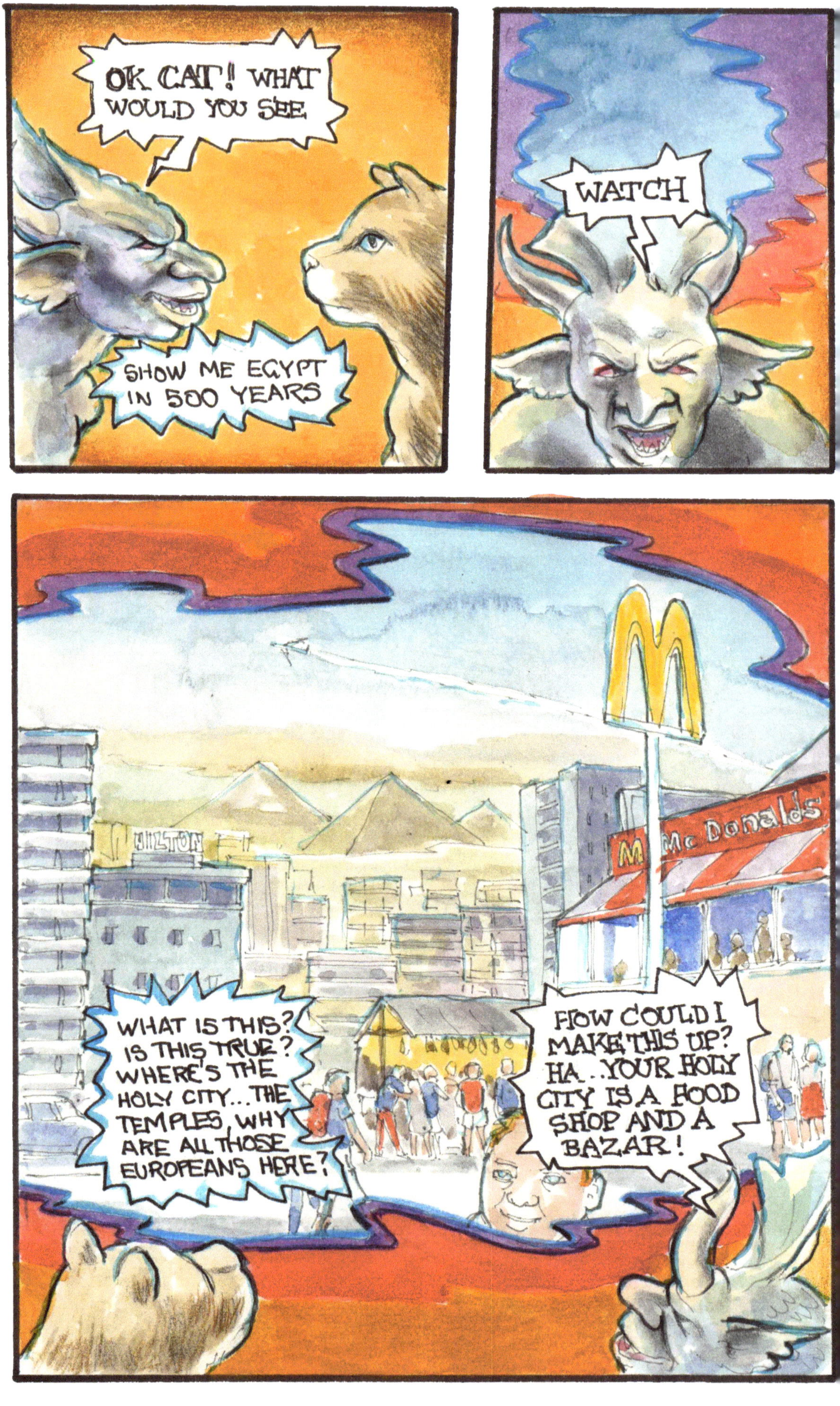

OK CAT! WHAT WOULD YOU SEE
SHOW ME EGYPT IN 500 YEARS

WATCH



McDonalds
WHAT IS THIS? IS THIS TRUE? WHERE'S THE HOLY CITY...THE TEMPLES, WHY ARE ALL THOSE EUROPEANS HERE?
HOW COULD I MAKE THIS UP? HA...YOUR HOLY CITY IS A FOOD SHOP AND A BAZAR!

HAVE YOU SEEN WHAT YOU WISHED?
SO BEGONE NOW DEMON, I BANISH YOU... BACK TO THE PITS OF HELL!
YES...
HA..HA.. TILL NEXT TIME WITCH, YOU'LL MISS ME..
I ALWAYS FEEL LIKE I NEED A BATH AFTER I DEAL WITH A DEMON
WHAT NOW CAT? HMM?
NOW I MUST RETURN TO MY MISTRESS..WILL YOU ACCOMPANY ME FURTHER?

LET ME THINK... STAY IN EUROPE WHERE EVERYONE SEEMS TO WANT TO KILL ME?
OF COURSE I'LL COME!
OR TRAVEL TO AN EXOTIC PLACE AND MAYBE MEET A GOD?
ME TOO I GUESS, I'VE NEVER BEEN TO EGYPT...
THEN, LET US FIND A SHIP..
END CHAPTER TWO

CHAPTER THREE

THAT DEMON WAS PRETTY NASTY..

DO YOU OFTEN HAVE TO SUMMON DEMONS?

NO.. ONLY IF I REALLY HAVE TO... OR WHEN I'M BORED

COULDN'T YOU HAVE ORGANISED CABINS FOR US?
WE HAD ONE GOLD COIN - I WAS LUCKY TO GET US ABOARD
BE THANKFUL BOY, I'VE HELD THAT COIN IN MY MOUTH SINCE I LEFT HOME... NO POCKETS YOU SEE

GIVE US YOUR MONEY GIRL..
I'VE GOT NONE!
I'M SURE THERE'S SUMAT ELSE YOU CAN GIVE US ALL

WHAT?
CRACK

AAARG!
WACK
THUMP SQEEZE
THUMP
GASP
ROAR!
RIP

ALRIGHT MISS.. STEP BACK..


I SAW WHAT HAPPENED BUT NOW TWO OF MY CREW ARE DEAD, ANOTHER USELESS FOR DAYS.. IF I WAS TO TURN YOU INTO THE JUSTICES YOUR CAT WOULD BE KILLED AND YOU'D DO TIME AT LEAST.. DEAD IS DEAD WHATEVER THE CIRCUMSTANCES

IF, AS YOU SAID, YOU SAW EVERYTHING, THEN WHY DIDN'T YOU STOP THEM?

OH, THEY WERE JUST HAVING A LITTLE FUN
YOUR IDEA OF FUN IS VERY DIFFERENT THAN MINE !!



BE THAT AS IT MAY, I SAW YOU DEFENDING YOUR SELF...
BUT THE JUSTICES WON'T SEE THAT !.. I BELIEVE I'M A FAIR MAN..SO I'VE DECIDED TO PUT YOU ASHORE AND SAY NO MORE OF THIS

EGYPT IS THAT WAY HA, HA

HA HA HA, YES.. THROUGH ABOUT 1500 MILES OF EMPTY DESERT! HA!



I READ TRUTH AND YET...SOME DECEIT IN THE CAPTAINS MIND

ZZZZLE

CRACK

CRASH!

BLAM

CRUNCH!

OWWW!

WHAT JUST HAPPENED? YOU BROKE THEIR SHIP AND THEIR BOAT, BUT THEN?...

THAT'S THE WAY MAGIC WORKS.. WHAT YOU DO TO OTHER WILL BE DONE TO YOU TOO...

WELL ... LET'S GET WALKING!.. IT SOUNDS LIKE A LONG WALK

WE WILL NOT GET FAR IN THIS SUN, WE MUST FIND WATER TOO
THE SUN IS AT IT'S ZENITH, WALK WITH ME TO THAT HIGH GROUND

FATHER RA...WE SEEK YOUR SUCCOUR...HELP US ON OUR JOURNEY TO MOTHER EGYPT...

END CHAPTER THREE

CHAPTER FOUR
AHH. WELCOME BACK MY GOOD SERVANT WHO ARE THESE?
THEY ARE FRIENDS I MET IN FRANCE... THEY HELPED ME IN MY QUEST

AND, WHAT DID YOU FIND OUT?

THE FUTURE LOOKS BAD FOR THE GODS, EGYPT BECOMES A CIRCUS..
HOW CAN YOU BE SURE..

THE WITCH HECATE SUMMONED A DEMON AND I SAW THE FUTURE, THERE WAS NO RESPECT, NO REVERENCE FOR THE OLDER GODS..
IS THIS TRUE WITCH?

ALL I SAW WAS A PLACE FULL OF FORIGNERS AND CHEAP FOOD AND NIC NAC BOOTHS

I DO NOT SENSE THE END FOR THE GODS... PERHAPS WHAT YOU SAW IS THE START OF THE OLDER GODS WAY DOWN....

WITCH! WILL YOU AND YOUR BOY DO SOMETHING FOR THE GODS?
WHAT?
BOY?
I WANT TO SEND YOU INTO THE FUTURE, A THOUSAND YEARS! TO SEE IF THE HUMANS STILL WORSHIP ME AND THE OTHER GODS!
WE MUST KNOW, HAVE THE HUMANS FORGOTTEN US?
I'LL GO..
ME TOO I GUESS..

YOU WERE VERY QUICK TO SAY YOU'D GO
IT'S AN ADVENTURE

I AM SENDING A MAU WITH YOU, SHE CAN COMMUNICATE WITH ME THROUGH THE UNDERWORLD, THE SHADOW REALM IS OUTSIDE TIME
BE PREPARED...YOU WILL ARRIVE IN THE AIR ABOVE THE HOLY NILE...

ZZZZZZ
ZZZZZZT

BLIP!

SPLOSH!

YOU OK?
YES, THIS LITTLE CAT IS ALL WET THOUGH..

THIS WATER SMELLS BAD! WHY DID BAST SEND THIS SILLY LITTLE CAT WITH US NOT OUR PUMA FRIEND



I DON'T KNOW, PERHAPS THIS CAT HAS SOME SPECIAL TRICKS
HISSSS...WELL MONKEY BOY AND GIRL...I DO HAVE ONE TRICK..I'M NOT DEAF OR STUPID LIKE SOME!

THE PUMA COULDN'T COME, HE IS TOO OLD, TIME SHIFTING TAKES ITS TOLE, IF HE CAME HE WOULDN'T BE ABLE TO GO BACK
FOLLOW ME, I'LL TAKE YOU TO THE TEMPLE DISTRICT

THE AIR HERE SMELLS LIKE SMOKE AND TURPENTINE

THE PEOPLE ALL SEEM ILL

CAREFUL..
ROARRR

THAT BLACK GLASSY HOLE IN THE GROUND WAS THE HOLY TEMPLES

WE WONT FIND MUCH HERE
LET'S WALK INTO THE SURROUNDING DISTRICT

I SEE NO SIGN OF ANY GODS HERE

WAIT...
SNIFF SNIFF
FOLLOW ME!



uncle yuri's
عرض عريب
מופע מזרחיות
freak show!
uncle yuris
IN HERE? REALLY?

HERE, LET US GO IN
GIVE HIM ONE OF THE COINS BAST GAVE YOU..
GOLD! I CAN'T CHANGE THAT, BUT IF YOU INSIST... GO, GO, GO IN! GO GO
IN THE BACK
BUBLE HEAD BOY AGE 23 FROM THE 2320 SINO-INDIAN WAR
LOBST AGE 1 FROM T EURO

THE AMAZING
DOG HEADED BOY
ON ... DATE
WHO ARE YOU?
I AM THE GREAT GOD ANUBIS
HMM.. NOT SO GREAT ANYMORE
GRRRRR...
WHAT HAPPENED? I THOUGHT YOU'D BE MUCH BIGGER
HA! ... I WAS, WITH NO BELIEF GODS SHRINK, DIMINISH..

WHY DON'T YOU ESCAPE FROM HERE?

TWO REASONS... ALL THE OTHER OLDER GODS ARE DEAD.. THEY LOST ALL THEIR BELIEVERS..

THERE'S BIG GAPS BETWEEN THE BARS..

AND EVEN THOUGH THE PEOPLE THAT COME TO SEE ME HERE DON'T KNOW I'M A GOD, THEY DO BELIEVE I EXIST, SO THAT LITTLE BELIEF KEEPS ME FROM DEATH

THE OTHER REASON IS; IF I STEP BETWEEN THE BARS, SEVERAL SECURITY ROBOTS ARRIVE...YOU CAN'T FIGHT OR REASON WITH THEM

I THINK I CAN HELP WITH THE GUARDS

LET'S TRY, STEP THROUGH

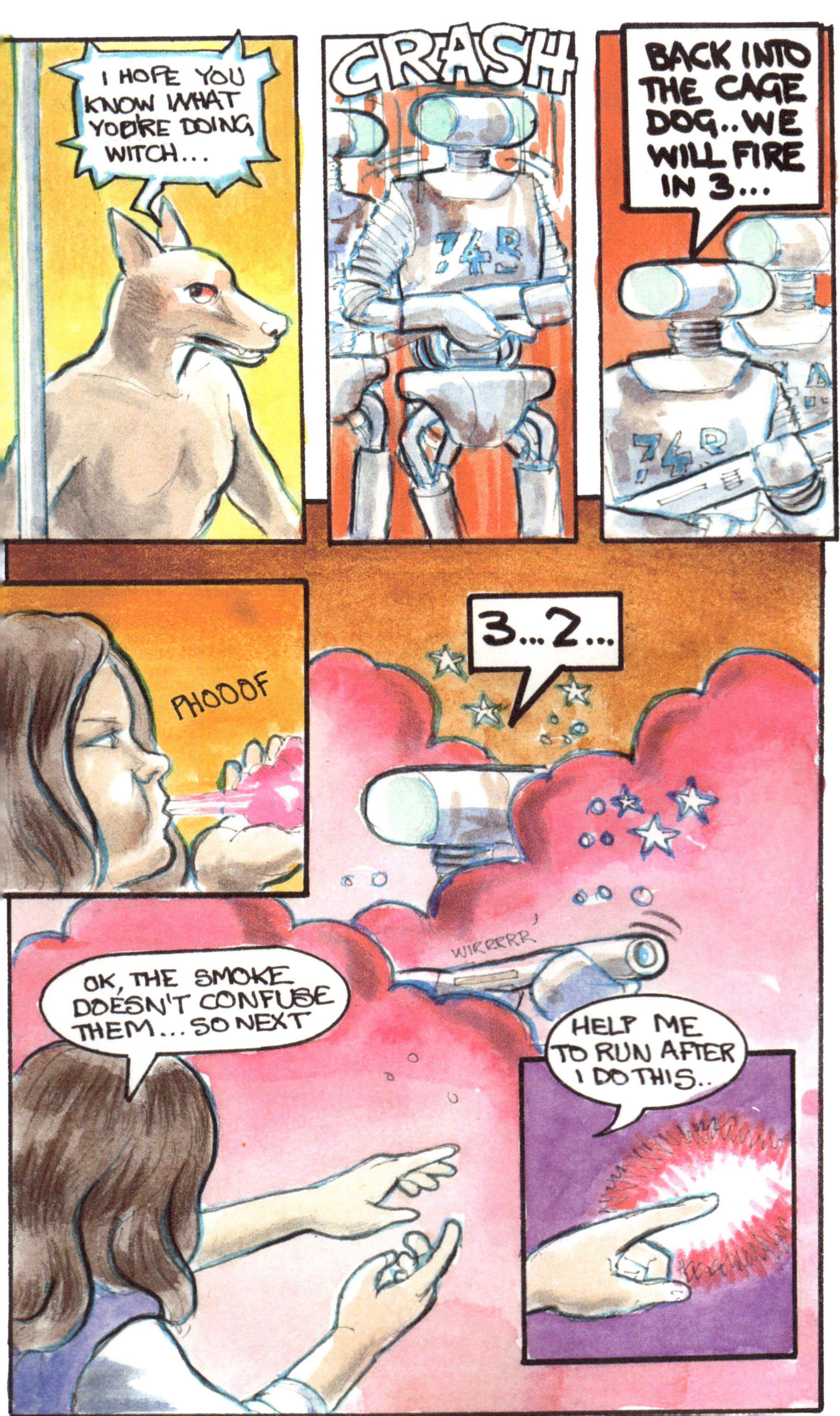
I HOPE YOU KNOW WHAT YOU'RE DOING WITCH...
CRASH
BACK INTO THE CAGE DOG .. WE WILL FIRE IN 3...
3...2...
PHOOOF
WIRRRRR
OK, THE SMOKE DOESN'T CONFUSE THEM... SO NEXT
HELP ME TO RUN AFTER I DO THIS..

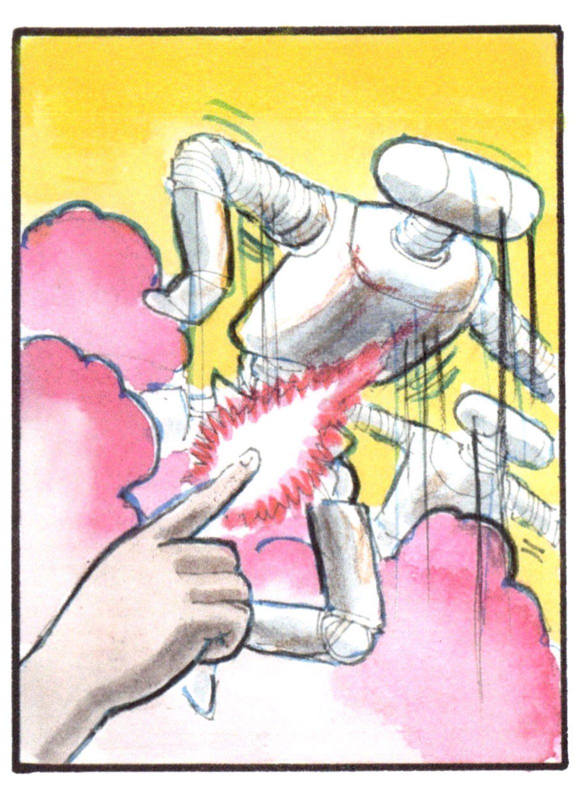

SLAM!

OOOF
WHAM!
QUICK..HELP ME UP BEFORE THEY FALL BACK..
OH..IT'S LIKE YOU WEIGH A THOUSAND POUNDS

I PROBABLY DO WEIGH THAT MUCH, I GET THE ROBOTS' WEIGHT SO I CAN SEND THEM TO THE CEILING!
I'VE TRIED THAT, I DON'T HAVE THE MASS TO LAY ON THEM.. THEY COULD EASILY CARRY MY WEIGHT
WOULDN'T IT HAVE BEEN..UM EASIER, TO THROW THEM ON THE FLOOR?
BESIDES, I END UP BOBBING IN THE AIR LIKE A BALLOON..
NOW WE ARE AWAY FROM THERE, WHAT CAN WE DO?
ANUBIS! HOW LITTLE YOU HAVE BECOME
WAIT HUMAN, I'M GOING TO TALK TO BAST..
IN THIS TIME YOU ARE DEAD SO DON'T BE TOO SMART

THEN I WILL SEND YOU ALL BACK TO THE TIME WHEN WE STILL HAD POWER AND YOU CAN TELL US WHAT TO DO..
THAT WOULD BE AROUND 2100...
SO BE IT.. BE READY TO SWIM
END CHAPTER FOUR

CHAPTER FIVE
WHY DO WE ALWAYS END UP IN THE RIVER
IF YOU ARRIVE ON LAND YOU MIGHT ARRIVE INSIDE A ROCK, THINGS MOVE ABOUT ON THE LAND LESS SO IN THE RIVER
LET US GO TO THE TEMPLES, I DON'T REMEMBER ANY OF THIS, I DON'T REMEMBER MUCH BEFORE ABOUT 2300

COKE
GOLD DRINKS
HOT DO
COOL COSTUME MAN..
CLICK CLICK CLICK
THERE IS NO REVERENCE HERE, LET US GO TO THE UNDERCROFT

PRESS HERE?
CLICK

RUMBLE

AH! MUCH BETTER
ANUBIS! YOU'RE DEAD! HOW ARE YOU BACK?

AH!..THAT EXPLAINS SOMETHING..I WONDERED HOW YOU COULD HAVE COME HERE IF YOU WERE ALREADY HERE...
YOU ARE HERE NOW NOW - FROM THE FUTURE, BUT YOUR'E NOT HERE NOW.. YOU ARE IN A LOOP OF TIME.. INTERESTING
WHAT? I DON'T UNDERSTAND?
DON'T WORRY, GO AND TALK TO THE OTHER GODS
BROTHERS, SISTERS, I HAVE RETURNED HERE FROM 2520...WHERE YOU ARE ALL DEAD!
WHAT!?
DEAD?
WHAT?
NO!
NO!
LISTEN, WE MUST GET PEOPLE TO BELIEVE IN US AGAIN OR WE ALL WILL DIE! HIDING DOWN HERE IS KILLING YOU, PEOPLE MUST SEE YOU TO BELIEVE IN YOU!

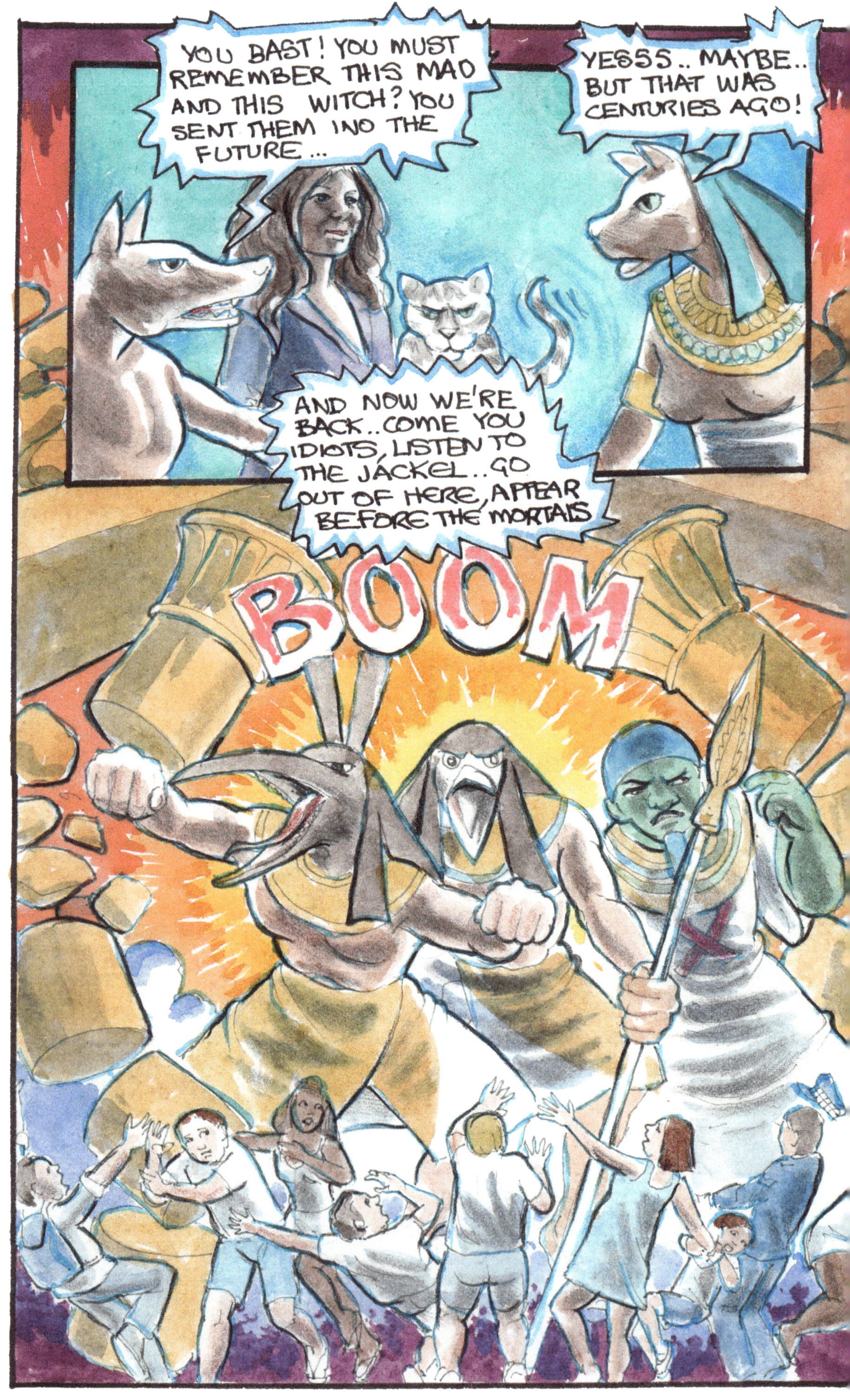

YOU BAST! YOU MUST REMEMBER THIS MAD AND THIS WITCH? YOU SENT THEM INO THE FUTURE...
YESSS.. MAYBE... BUT THAT WAS CENTURIES AGO!
AND NOW WE'RE BACK..COME YOU IDIOTS, LISTEN TO THE JACKEL..GO OUT OF HERE, APPEAR BEFORE THE MORTALS
BOOM

BOOM! CRASH
WE ARE THE OLDER GODS!
WE HAVE RETURNED!
BOOM
FEAR ME!

WHAT ARE THEY DOING! DON'T THEY WANT PEOPLE TO WORSHIP THEM?
IT'S NOT THAT SIMPLE, THE GODS DON'T CARE IF THEY WORSHIP THEM, IT'S JUST BELIEF THEY ARE AFTER



STOP! STOP! THEY ARE INNOCENT PEOPLE
DOESN'T MATTER WE NEED THEIR FEAR, LOVE OR HATE, IT'S ALL THE SAME, ALL BELIEF STARTS WITH FEAR!
GODS ARE SUPPOSED TO CARE FOR THEIR FOLLOWERS... YOU DON'T DESERVE TO SURVIVE!

I CAN'T GET MY MAGIC TO WORK ON THESE GODS!
DON'T BE TOO ANGRY AT THEM, THEY ARE WHAT PEOPLE MADE THEM
NO, IT CAN'T, THEY AREN'T PHYSICAL THEY'RE SOLID DREAMS
WHAT DO YOU MEAN
WHERE DO YOU THINK GODS COME FROM? PEOPLE NEED SOMETHING TO EXPLAIN THE THUNDER.. SO THEY INVENT A GOD...
ONCE ENOUGH PEOPLE BELIEVE THE GOD BECOMES REAL, THAT IS WHY THEY NEED OUR BELIEF, IT IS OUR BELIEF THAT MAKES THEM...
BOOM
BUT THEYR'E NOT SMART, PEOPLE IMAGINED BIG AND POWERFUL.. BUT NOT INTELLIGENT...
MOST OF THESE COULDN'T FIND THEIR BUMS WITH BOTH HANDS
BUT.. STILL...
CRACK
I KNOW, I KNOW, BAST IS BETTER THAN MOST, SHE HAS BEEN TASKED WITH MINDING PEOPLE AND HAS LEARNED SOME EMPATHY

BOOM!
BOOM!
RAT TAT TAT
KER-ACK!
YOU DARE CHALLENGE YOUR GODS?
I TRIED TO STOP THE OTHER GODS FROM HURTING PEOPLE... THEY DON'T SEE THESE AREN'T THE SUPERSTITIOUS PEASANTS THEY REMEMBER...
WAIT... I REMEMBER ALL THIS.. OH NO... RUN!

BOOM
ZIP ZIP
CRUNCH

ZEEEE
BLIP
ROAR!

AH... LOOK! THEY FLEE BEFORE US..

NOO... WE MUST RUN
SEE BOY...I FORESAW YOU WOULD HAVE A JOB TO DO..

ROAR
BOOOM
WELL.. AT LEAST NOW WE KNOW WHAT CAUSED THE BIG HOLE...
I'M SORRY WITCH BOY, WE ARE ALL STUCK HERE, THE GOD'S HAVE LITTLE POWER LEFT
THAT'S OK I WANT TO SEE WHAT HAPPENS NEXT
THE END - FOR NOW

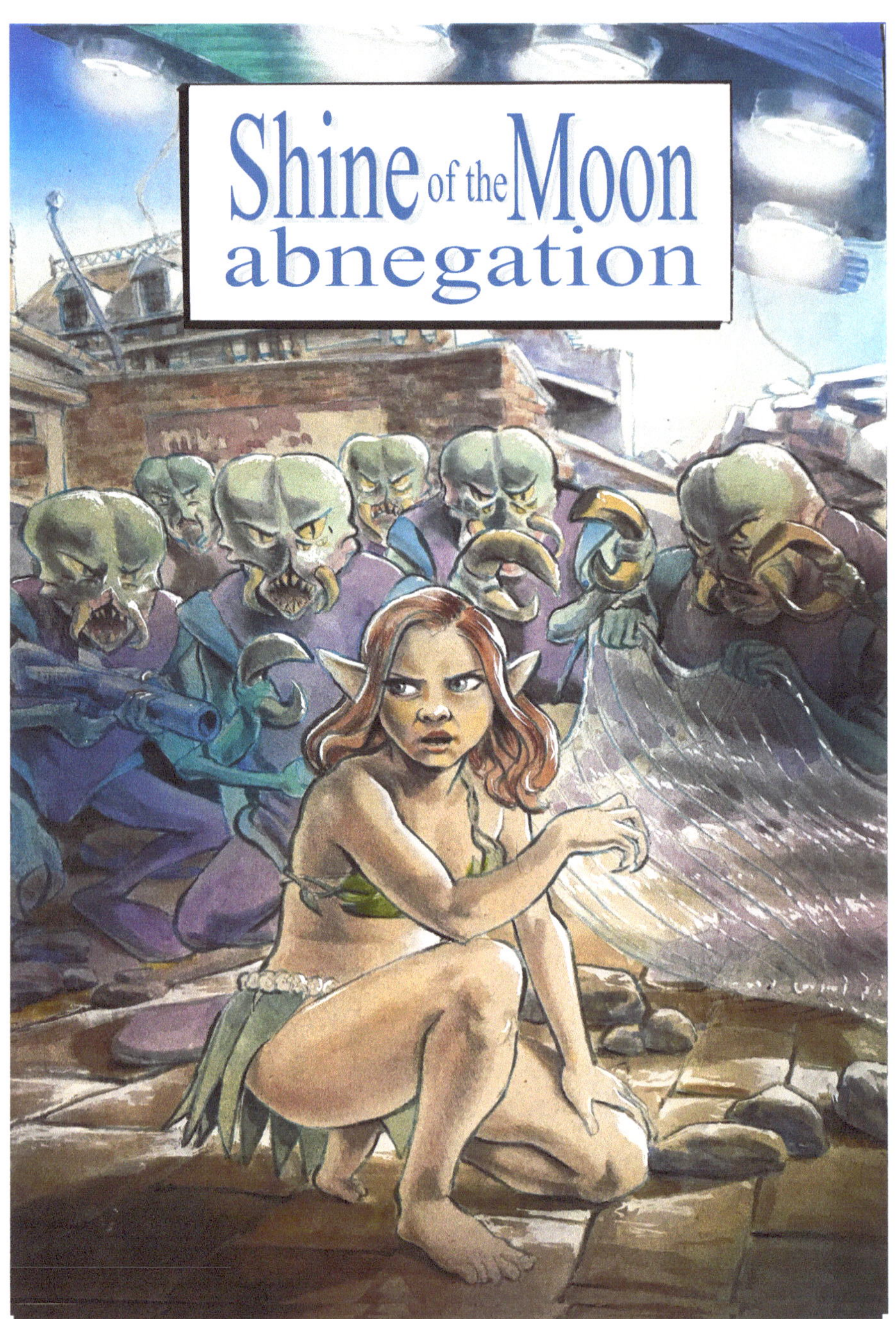

Shine of the Moon
abnegation
COMING SOON
FOR DETAILS OR TO ORDER VISIT johnlawryart.com